K

TOWNSHIP PUBLIC LIBRARY

3 2170 03036965 2

DATE DU

MAR 22 2017

D066170·4

ITCH
WN

STONE ARCH BOOKS
a capstone imprint

You Choose Stories: Scooby-Doo
is published by Stone Arch Books,
A Capstone Imprint
1710 Roe Crest Drive
North Mankato, Minnesota 56003
www.mycapstone.com

Copyright © 2017 Hanna-Barbera.
SCOOBY-DOO and all related characters and elements
are trademarks of © Hanna-Barbera.
WB SHIELD: ™ & © Warner Bros. Entertainment Inc.
(s17)

CAPS37490

All rights reserved. No part of this publication may be
reproduced in whole or in part, or stored in a retrieval
system, or transmitted in any form or by any means,
electronic, mechanical, photocopying, recording, or
otherwise, without written permission of the publisher.

Cataloging-in-Publication Data is available on the
Library of Congress website.
ISBN: 978-1-4965-4334-9 [Library Hardcover]
ISBN: 978-1-4965-4336-3 [paperback]
ISBN: 978-1-4965-4338-7 [eBook PDF]
ISBN: 978-1-4965-5389-8 [reflowable epub]

Summary: Scooby-Doo and the rest of Mystery Inc. are
invited to be judges at an annual Halloween costume
contest in Salem, Massachusetts.

Printed in Canada.
10050S17

SCOOBY-DOO!

THE SALEM WITCH SHOWDOWN

written by
Matthew K. Manning

illustrated by
Scott Neely

THE MYSTERY INC. GANG!

SCOOBY-DOO

SKILLS: Loyal; super snout
BIO: This happy-go-lucky hound avoids scary situations at all costs, but he'll do anything for a Scooby Snack!

SHAGGY ROGERS

SKILLS: Lucky; healthy appetite
BIO: This laid-back dude would rather look for grub than search for clues, but he usually finds both!

FRED JONES JR.

SKILLS: Athletic; charming
BIO: The leader and oldest member of the gang. He's a good sport — and good at them, too!

DAPHNE BLAKE

SKILLS: Brains; beauty
BIO: As a sixteen-year-old fashion queen, Daphne solves her mysteries in style.

VELMA DINKLEY

SKILLS: Clever; highly intelligent
BIO: Although she's the youngest member of Mystery Inc., Velma's an old pro at catching crooks.

← YOU CHOOSE →

SCOOBY-DOO!

™

Someone — or something — doesn't want the
Mystery Inc. gang in Salem. But who or what
is behind the spooky appearances at the high
school's annual costume contest? Only YOU can
help Scooby-Doo and the rest of Mystery Inc.
decide *witch* way to go to solve the mystery.

Follow the directions at the bottom of each page.
The choices YOU make will change the outcome
of the story. After you finish one path, go
back and read the others for more Scooby-Doo
adventures!

YOU CHOOSE the path to solve . . .

THE SALEM WITCH
SHOWDOWN

"S-S-Salem?!?!" Shaggy says from the back of the Mystery Machine.

"That's right," Daphne replies from the front seat. She looks back at her lanky friend and his Great Dane, Scooby-Doo. Both are visibly shivering. It's not an unusual look for the pair, but Daphne smiles just the same.

"Like, the same Salem where they had that major witch problem?" Shaggy says.

"If you're referring to the historical Salem Witch Trials of the 1690s, then yes, that's it exactly," says Velma as the van comes to a stop.

"C'mon, guys," says Fred from the behind the wheel. He turns off the Mystery Machine and opens his door. "It's not a big deal. We were asked to be guest judges at their high school's annual Halloween costume contest. That's it. It's an honor, really."

Turn the page.

Fred steps outside and walks around to the back of the van, opening the door for Shaggy and Scooby-Doo. But when he peers inside, there's no trace of either of them.

Daphne and Velma walk to the back of the Mystery Machine too. Velma looks in the open door. "I can see you under that blanket," she says.

While Scooby and Shaggy had done a fairly good job hiding behind the gang's luggage, the blanket they're hiding under is shaking uncontrollably. It makes it fairly easy for Velma to uncover their hiding place.

"Like, we're not coming out!" says Shaggy.

"Reah!" agrees Scooby.

The two lumps under the blanket begin shaking more than ever.

"Guess we'll just have to go to the costume party without you guys," says Fred.

"It's a shame all that candy will go to waste," says Daphne. She, Fred, and Velma turn toward the school and begin walking to its entrance.

"C-c-c-candy?" stutters one of the lumps under the blanket.

"Sure!" Velma calls. "The invitation says the judges get free access to the treat table."

The Mystery Inc. gang reaches the school's double doors, and Daphne pulls one open. Suddenly, a dark shadow falls over her.

Daphne lets out a gasp and whips around. But it's none other than Scooby and Shaggy standing directly behind her.

"Did someone say treat table?" Shaggy asks.

"Geez, guys," says Daphne. "Cool it on the dramatic entrances, will you?"

"Just be glad they're here," says Velma. "We're late enough already."

"No, you're right on time," a gruff voice says from inside the school. "If it is you, of course."

The person standing in the doorway is a tall, older gentleman. His forehead is wrinkled with age, and his large eyebrows have been whitened by the same process.

Turn the page.

"You must be Principal Hawthorne," says Velma.

"That's correct," the man replies. "And you must be Mystery Inc."

"That's us," says Fred, smiling.

The principal doesn't smile back. He simply turns and walks down a hall toward another set of double doors. "This way, please," he says. "Let's get this over with."

The Mystery Inc. gang follows him into the school's auditorium. The entire room is decorated with fake cobwebs, cutout ghosts, goblins, and large black paper cats.

There are rows upon rows of chairs fixed to the floor, all filled with a variety of monsters and other fiendish faces. The gang spots Frankenstein's Monster, a few vampires, a large cardboard robot, and plenty of witches — way too many witches for Shaggy's taste.

"Like, this place is crawling with creeps," Shaggy says.

"Be nice," says Daphne. "It's a costume contest. What did you expect?"

"I don't know," says Shaggy. "Superheroes? Cartoon characters? People dressed up like cuddly teddy bears?"

"This is Salem," says Velma. "They take Halloween here very seriously."

"As well we should," Principal Hawthorne adds. "Why don't you head up to your table?" He points across the room to a long table lining the side of the auditorium's stage.

Fred and Daphne start for the stage, but Velma hangs back. "What did you mean earlier?" she asks, looking at Principal Hawthorne. "When you asked if it was really us this time?"

"Yeah," says Shaggy. "Like, who else would it be?"

Turn the page.

"Like, us," says a voice from the back row of seats.

Shaggy looks over to the source of the sound, only to see a mirror image of the Mystery Inc. gang. "Hey," he says, "you're us!"

"No," says the young man dressed just like Shaggy. "You're *us*."

Beside the fake Shaggy are three other teens. They're dressed just like Fred, Daphne, and Velma. Next to them is a dog dressed just like Scooby-Doo. If Shaggy didn't know better, he'd swear he's looking in a mirror.

"Awesome costumes, you guys," says Fred. "You're not going to make it easy on us judges."

Just then, the lights go out!

If the gang retreats back outside, go to page 13.

If the gang hunts for a light, turn to page 14.

If the gang stays put, turn to page 16.

Scooby and Shaggy can't move their legs fast enough. The auditorium is pitch black, and the two can't see anything in front of them. But that doesn't stop them from running.

In a flurry, they collide with the auditorium's double doors, shoving them open. They race down the hall and outside to the early evening air. A few minutes later, the rest of Mystery Inc. runs outside after them.

"Whoa, guys," says Fred. "Slow down."

"Yeah," says Velma. "Why the quick exit?"

Shaggy stops in the parking lot. He turns to face his friends. Scooby-Doo does the same.

"What do you mean, why?" says Shaggy. "You want to stay inside in a dark room full of, like, ghosts and goblins?"

"Better than being out here!" shouts Daphne as she points to the sky. Behind Shaggy and Scooby are three witches flying through the air on broomsticks!

If the gang follows the witches, turn to page 18.

If the gang runs away from the witches, turn to page 25.

"There's got to be a light switch around here someplace," says Velma.

Scooby and Shaggy don't answer. Aside from their teeth chattering, they're too scared to make a sound.

That's not the case for the rest of the auditorium, however. The ghouls, ghosts, and goblins are all abuzz. With the doors closed, there is zero light in the auditorium. While Shaggy and Scooby-Doo stay put, the others try to find their way in the darkness.

"Found the wall," says Fred.

"Me too," says Daphne.

"Me, three," says Velma.

"Hey!" says an unfamiliar voice.

"Jinkies!" says Velma.

"I'm not a wall," says the voice.

Just then the lights turn on. Daphne is standing by the door, next to the light switch. Velma looks at the young man in the giant cardboard box in front of her.

"I'm supposed to be a killer robot," says the boy in the box.

"Like, I wouldn't worry about the guy dressed as a refrigerator," says Shaggy.

"Killer robot!" the young man corrects, a bit angrier this time.

"Like, we should be worried about those guys instead!" Shaggy says, pointing up at the rafters.

Fred, Daphne, Velma, and Scooby-Doo all look up toward the ceiling. There, three witches are circling the room on broomsticks. Each is clad in a black robe and matching pointed hat.

"How is that even possible?" says Velma under her breath.

"How is it possible that we haven't run out of here?!" yells Shaggy.

Suddenly, the witches fly to the stage and disappear in the curtains.

"Let's follow them!" shouts Fred. "If we don't find those witches, the contest will be ruined!"

"No, let's do the opposite of that thing you just said," says Shaggy. "I'm going downstairs to hide!"

To follow Scooby-Doo and Shaggy downstairs, turn to page 21.

To follow Fred, Daphne, and Velma upstairs, turn to page 27.

"Nobody move," says Fred. It's hard to hear him over the commotion of the room. The vampires, ghosts, goblins, and witches all seem to like the dark less than expected.

Suddenly a scream erupts from the stage. Shaggy and Scooby hug each other out of sheer terror. And just like that, the lights turn back on.

"Um, excuse me?" says a teenager dressed like Frankenstein's Monster. Shaggy has his arms wrapped around him, mistaking him for his familiar Great Dane.

"Do we know each other?" says a girl dressed like a witch. Scooby-Doo has her in a bear hug.

"Like, sorry!" Shaggy says, peeling himself off the Frankenstein Monster.

"Rorry!" Scooby-Doo agrees.

"The prize money!" says Principal Hawthorne from the stage. "It's gone!"

Mystery Inc. rushes to the stage. Principal Hawthorne is holding an empty envelope — one that had been resting on the judges' table.

"How much was in there?" asks Velma.

"Five hundred dollars," says the principal. "After the decorations, and the treat table and such, it's all we had left in the budget."

"I told you this sort of thing would happen, Hawthorne," says a woman from the front row of seats. "I want a word with you."

"Who's that?" Daphne whispers to Velma.

"That's city councilwoman Nancy Spindle," says Velma. "I recognize her from the Salem government website."

"Oh, man!" says Shaggy. "Somebody better go check to make sure the treats are OK!"

"We need to shut down the room," says Fred. "We'll conduct a formal investigation."

"But the treats!" says Shaggy. "Won't someone think of the treats!"

To interview the suspects with Daphne, Fred, and Velma, turn to page 23.

To check on the treat table with Scooby and Shaggy, turn to page 29.

The three bizarre figures hovering in the late afternoon air turn away from the Mystery Inc. gang. They head toward downtown Salem.

"After them!" shouts Fred, as he runs in the direction of the witches.

"After them?" says Shaggy. "Like, after the terrifying women flying on magic sticks? You're as crazy as they are!"

But as Shaggy and Scooby look around they realize no one is listening. Fred, Daphne, and Velma have all begun sprinting toward the center of town.

Scooby-Doo and Shaggy take a moment to look at each other with wide eyes. They don't want to follow the witches. But they also don't want to be standing in an empty parking lot where witches like to hang out. They didn't even want to be in Salem in the first place!

Shaggy swallows, making an audible **GULP**. They have no choice. He and Scooby chase after their friends.

By the time Scooby and Shaggy catch up to the gang, the witches are nowhere in sight.

"Oh, good, you lost them!" says Shaggy.

Daphne and Velma glare at their skinny friend in the green shirt.

"I mean, oh, rats," Shaggy says unconvincingly.

"They went over there," says Velma. She points toward a nearby two-story building. A sign in front says *Salem Wax Museum*.

"Reepy," Scooby mutters under his breath.

"You said it, old pal," says Shaggy.

"OK, let's go," says Fred.

"We're gonna pass," says Shaggy. "I think . . . I think they went over there." He points across the street to a building with a sign that says *Pirate Museum*.

"Reah," says Scooby, nodding his head in agreement. "Rirates!"

"I guess we're splitting up," says Daphne.

To follow Fred, Daphne, and Velma, turn to page 32.
To follow Scooby and Shaggy, turn to page 48.

"Follow witches," Shaggy says as he and Scooby-Doo walk into the hall outside the auditorium. "What kind of crazy talk is that?"

"Razy," Scooby agrees.

"Those witches looked like they were heading up, so we go down," says Shaggy.

"Rokay!" says Scooby, nodding his head. He and Shaggy walk down a nearby set of stairs and then into a dark hallway.

"Huh," says Shaggy. "This is kinda spookier than I thought it'd be."

"Reah," Scooby agrees. He does his best to hide behind Shaggy as the two slowly move to a door at the end of the hall.

It takes the pair about twice as long as it should, but they finally reach the door.

"You go first," says Shaggy.

"Ruh-uh," says Scooby-Doo. He shakes his head no, as if to make his point even clearer.

Turn the page.

The two finally pull the door open at the same time. It creaks on its hinges, and a faint moan echoes across the room. Scooby jumps into Shaggy's arms.

"Well, that couldn't have been much creepier," says Shaggy, setting Scooby-Doo down.

The two make their way into the dark room. Shaggy flips a light switch near the door.

"Oh," he says. "It's just a locker room."

They look around the room. Dusty old lockers line the wall. They look as if they haven't been used in decades. There's a wooden door at the opposite end of the room, but it looks to be boarded up.

"See, Scoobs," says Shaggy. "I told you. Nothing to be afraid —"

Shaggy doesn't have time to finish his sentence. He's interrupted by the sound of the door behind him slamming shut.

Scooby tries the door. It's locked.

If Shaggy and Scooby-Doo scream for help, turn to page 34.
If they search for another way out, turn to page 52.

"I didn't even know there was going to be prize money," says a young man in a vampire costume. "How much was it?"

"That's . . . don't worry about it," says Velma with a sigh. She isn't getting any useful information out of the teenaged suspects in the room.

Velma looks over at Fred, who is busy interviewing the fake Mystery Inc. They're now sitting near the front of the stage.

"Huh," Velma says out loud.

"I can't go to jail!" shouts the excited vampire. "I'm too weak and frail! My mom always says so! I bruise easily! Like a banana."

Velma sighs again and walks away from the easily excited king of the undead. "Fred," she says to her friend. "A word?"

Fred excuses himself from the Mystery Inc. look-alikes and walks over to the base of the stage with Velma.

Turn the page.

"When the lights went out," Velma says, "we were standing right next to those Mystery Inc. copycats. Now they're by the stage. You don't find that odd?"

"Maybe they tried to get out of the room when the lights were off," Fred suggests.

"Or maybe they nabbed the prize money," says Velma.

"Well, if they had it, they don't now," Fred says. "Look."

Principal Hawthorne is at the auditorium doors next to Councilwoman Spindle. As the students get to the head of the line, they empty out their pockets, as well as their bags, in front of the two.

The fake Mystery Inc. teens are exiting the line. Having been checked, they leave the auditorium.

"Hmm," says Velma. Just then a group of witches pass the principal.

"Wait," says Fred. "He's not checking their hats."

The witches pass Principal Hawthorne and exit the room.

If the gang follows the fake Mystery Inc., turn to page 36.
If the gang follows the witches, turn to page 55.

Taking a cue from Shaggy and Scooby, the Mystery Inc. gang takes off. Soon they're running away from the witches as fast as they can.

Letting Shaggy and Scooby take the lead is never a good strategy for the gang, but right now, none of them are thinking clearly. If they were, they would have insisted that they head toward town, rather than toward the creepy country road Scooby and Shaggy are headed for. If the gang was thinking clearly, perhaps the witches would have decided not to follow them.

But the gang follows Shaggy and Scooby, and the witches follow the gang.

"They're getting closer," says Velma. She's the only one in the group brave enough to turn around and see if the witches are still there.

"Like, I told you Salem was a bad idea!" says Shaggy through panting breaths.

The witches are so close now that one of them swoops down on her broomstick toward Scooby, nearly snagging his tail.

Turn the page.

Scooby-Doo picks up speed, taking the lead. The road curves in front of him, lined by thick, dark woods on either side. The sun has set now, and away from downtown, it's quite hard to see. But Mystery Inc. keeps running, even as the sound of cackling fizzles out behind them.

Velma turns around again. The witches are nowhere to be seen.

"Guys!" she says, coming to a slow stop. "They're . . . they're gone."

While Shaggy and Scooby-Doo keep running for several more yards, Daphne and Fred stop near Velma. They turn to look behind them and see nothing but the evening air.

Fred turns back to the road and surveys their surroundings. In front of them stands a dark gas station that looks nearly abandoned. Next to it is an old, rickety covered wooden bridge.

"Where to now?" asks Daphne.

If the gang goes inside the gas station, turn to page **68**.
If the gang crosses the rickety bridge, turn to page **86**.

Fred, Daphne, and Velma race out of the auditorium and up the stairs.

"Where are we going?" asks Daphne.

"The way you'd go if you had the ability to fly on a broomstick," Velma replies. "Up — way up."

The three dart out of the stairwell at the second floor of the school. In front of them is a mostly empty hallway. The lights are off, since no students are expected to be on that level of the school.

"I don't see them anywhere," says Daphne.

The three friends walk down the hall, through an arched doorway. On the other side is a gymnasium. There is a set of wooden bleachers in front of them across the small basketball court.

"Still no sign of them," says Daphne. She's beginning to doubt Velma's instincts.

Nevertheless, the three walk out onto the gym floor.

"Hey!" shouts a voice from near the bleachers.

Turn the page.

"You're mucking up my floor," says a man with messy brown hair. He walks toward them, holding a mop in hand.

"Oh," says Daphne. "Sorry. We're just . . . have you seen anyone come through here?"

"I just started cleaning this room," the janitor replies. His gruff voice matches his features. "Some wise guys thought it was a good idea to set off their little volcano experiment in the chemistry lab. Got fake lava all over my floors. Just finished cleaning it now."

"Where does that go?" asks Fred, pointing to a small door on the side of the base of the wooden bleachers.

"It's nothing," says the janitor. "Goes nowhere."

"It's unlocked," says Velma. She pulls the door open, but can't see a thing inside. It's pitch black.

If the gang heads inside, turn to page 71.

If they leave the gym, turn to page 89.

While Velma, Fred, and Daphne stay in the auditorium, Shaggy and Scooby-Doo slip backstage behind the curtains. There, in the center of the small room used for quick changes during high school productions, is a long banquet table.

The table is stacked with donuts, bowls of candies, plates of cookies, and a dozen bottles of soda. There's even a small bowl of dog treats. It's the last thing Shaggy notices, but the first thing Scooby spies.

"Scooby Snacks!" Scooby says.

"This treat table," Shaggy says, "is the most beautiful thing I've ever laid eyes on."

"Reah," Scooby agrees.

The two look at each other and then back at the table. Then suddenly, they pounce.

Turn the page.

Face down in a bowl full of gummy worms, Shaggy doesn't see the painting hanging above the table. But Scooby can see it from the far end of the table as he shovels dog treats into his mouth.

The painting is of a woman in traditional witch garb. It looks old, like something rendered in the early days of the country. As Scooby studies it, the painting suddenly sneezes.

"Gesundheit," says Scooby-Doo. He gobbles two more Scooby Snacks before it dawns on him. He stops eating and looks back up at the painting. "Uh, Raggy?"

"What — *CHOMP!* — what's — *MUNCH!* — up, pal?" Shaggy manages to say between a fistful of donuts and a bite of brownie.

"The rainting," Scooby says, pointing to the portrait of the witch.

"Yeah — *CRUNCH!* — that's one — *CHOMP!* — creepy gal, that's for sure. *MUNCH!*" Shaggy says.

"Rit sneezed!" Scooby says.

If Scooby-Doo and Shaggy investigate the painting, turn to page 73.

If they ignore it and keep eating, turn to page 94.

Daphne pulls on the door of the wax museum. As it opens, a bell jingles. The man behind the counter looks up from his newspaper.

"Oh," he says as they come in, "I didn't expect to see anyone today."

"Hi," says Velma. "Did you happen to see any suspicious people come through here?"

"Describe 'suspicious,'" says the man behind the counter. "You're acting pretty suspicious right now."

The man's voice is gruff. His messy black hair and rigid, pointed eyebrows only add to his unwelcoming demeanor.

"Um . . .," Daphne says, almost embarrassed to describe who she's looking for. "Maybe dressed like witches?"

"Witches?" the man repeats. "No, I think I would remember seeing a band of witches."

"OK," says Velma. "Sorry to bother you." She takes Daphne by the hand and turns to leave the wax museum.

"Wait," says Daphne. She stops in the middle of the lobby. Her eyes focus on something just around the corner. She can barely make it out. "We'd like three tickets, please."

Fred and Velma look at their friend curiously.

Daphne nods at them and then to the man behind the front desk. "Three tickets," she says again.

"Good," the man replies, not bothering to smile. "At least somebody's going to skip that annoying costume party. Waste of time if you ask me." He tears three tickets off a cheap spool and hands them over. "That'll be fifteen dollars."

Turn to page 38.

"Help!" shouts Shaggy. "Like, somebody, anybody! Help!"

Shaggy's screaming is interrupted when Scooby-Doo pulls at his shirttail. "Risten!" the Great Dane says.

The two stay completely quiet for a moment. There's the sound of footsteps coming down the hall toward them.

"We're saved!" says Shaggy. "That is, unless —"

"Riches," Scooby-Doo says in a quiet voice.

"Gulp," Shaggy says.

There's a sound at the door, like someone fiddling with the latch. Then slowly the door creaks open.

"Oh, man," whispers Shaggy. "We're, like, doomed!"

Shaggy does his very best to hide behind Scooby-Doo, but the Great Dane is currently trying his best to hide behind Shaggy.

The door swings all the way open.

Standing in the doorway are Fred, Daphne, and Velma.

Scooby-Doo and Shaggy let out simultaneous sighs of relief.

"Man, am I glad to see you guys," says Shaggy.

"Reah!" Scooby agrees.

"We've been looking all over for you," says Daphne. "They're waiting for us to judge the costume contest."

"They're still going ahead with that thing?" says Shaggy.

"Yep," says Fred. "Seems those witches, or whatever they were, took off. No sign of them anywhere."

"You say that like it's a bad thing," says Shaggy.

He and Scooby attempt to regain their composure, and then follow their friends back toward the auditorium.

Turn to page 42.

After rounding up Daphne — and pulling Shaggy and Scooby-Doo away from the treat table backstage — Fred and Velma lead the gang outside. They see the fake Mystery Inc. gang walking on the nearby sidewalk. They're walking toward downtown Salem.

"There's something fishy about those guys," says Velma.

Keeping behind them a good pace so as not to draw attention, the real Mystery Inc. follows their doppelgängers across town to a public park. The fake gang walks into a picnic house and takes seats at a table.

Meanwhile, the real gang sneaks up to the back of the picnic house's solid wall. They crouch near the corner.

"Like, what are we doing?" whispers Shaggy.

"Shhh!" is the only response from all four of his friends.

"You know," whispers Shaggy, "sometimes I worry you guys don't value me as a member of this team."

"Shhh!" the others say again.

"Well, now I'm reassured," whispers Shaggy.

"So when is he getting here?" the fake Velma asks the other members of her fake gang.

"Any second now," fake Fred replies.

"Well, I hope so," says fake Shaggy. "I can't wait to spend my cut at that new gourmet tapas restaurant. I've heard it's a delight to the palate."

"Like, this guy does an awful me," the real Shaggy whispers from behind the wall. "Tapas are only good if you get like, a thousand of them."

"Shhh!" the gang says again.

"Hey, don't get mad at me," whispers Shaggy. "I'm not the actor giving the unconvincing performance."

"Here he comes," fake Daphne says to her friends. "I see his truck."

Turn to page 45.

"Why are we here?" Fred asks Daphne as soon as they're out of the earshot of the man behind the counter.

"He's too suspicious," says Daphne. "And I saw . . . these!"

As they turn the corner in the hallway, Fred and Velma see exactly what Daphne is talking about. On the floor of the first room in the wax museum is a pile of black clothing: robes, boots, and black pointy hats.

Velma picks up the robe on top of the pile. It's heavier than she expects it to be. She looks at the back of the neckline and sees a small metal pulley sewn into the loose piece of material. "Is this . . . ?"

"What the witches were wearing," Daphne finishes. "I saw one of the hats from the lobby."

"They're rigged up with pulleys," says Fred, stating the obvious.

"There must have been some sort of wire we couldn't see," says Velma. "Something they strung up in the air to make it look like they were flying."

"So we know the how," says Fred. "But not the who."

"Whoever it is," says Velma, "they couldn't have gotten far."

At that, Fred and Daphne look around the room. There are wax figures everywhere. Most are of celebrities and historical figures. They walk through the room into the next hall.

"Whoa!" Velma exclaims. "I knew the town had heard about us, but this is ridiculous."

In front of the gang stands wax figures of Fred, Velma, Daphne, Scooby-Doo, and Shaggy.

"They're so lifelike," says Fred. He reaches out to touch his doppelgänger. "The wax is even spongy."

Fred stares at the wax double. He looks deep into its eyes.

And that's when the wax Fred blinks.

Turn the page.

"You're pathetic," says a voice from the doorway. It's the man behind the counter.

"Hey!" says the wax Fred. "I was doing my best."

"You're working for the wax museum?" asks Fred. "Why?"

"Isn't it obvious?" says Velma. "They were hired to scare people away from the costume show. To drum up business here, I'm guessing."

The man puts his hand to his head, defeated. "I just wanted to attract new customers. It's not fair to have all these people in town and none of them coming here. The costume contest was ruining my business! I need to make a living!"

"What was in it for you?" Velma asks.

"Like, he promised us treats," says fake Shaggy.

Velma shakes her head. It all makes sense now.

"Like, do you think we still get treats, Scoob?" the fake Shaggy asks his canine best friend.

"Ri rope so," the fake Scooby-Doo replies.

THE END

To follow another path, turn to page 12.

Back in the auditorium, the gang takes their places at the table on the stage. Principal Hawthorne walks up the microphone at the center of the stage.

"All right," he says. "After a bit of a . . . delay . . . we're ready to get back on track. Group #1, please take the stage."

Fred, Daphne, and Velma watch as a group of four vampires parades around in front of them. The audience claps. One of the vampires trips on his cape, and the others help him up. They smile a bit nervously as they walk offstage and take their seats in the audience.

"Is it wrong to already be bored?" Shaggy whispers to Scooby.

"Group #2," says Principal Hawthorne. Frankenstein's Monster and his bride stumble onto the stage.

Shaggy looks at the line of kids behind them. He sees the fake Scooby-Doo and Shaggy up next with a group of ghosts behind them. The ghost costumes are pretty plain. They just look like three kids draped in bedsheets.

"Reat rable?" Scooby-Doo whispers to Shaggy.

"Yeah, old buddy," says Shaggy. "You've got a point. Where's the treat table?"

"Shhh!" says Velma.

"Group #3," says Principal Hawthorne. The fake Scooby and Shaggy take the stage.

"Like, where's the rest of 'em?" Shaggy says.

"Shhh!" Velma says. "We're trying to judge here."

"Like, excuuuuuuuse me," says Shaggy. "First we're lured here with the promise of a treat table, and then we're forced to watch cheap pretenders parade around like us onstage."

"Well, I think these two are great," says Velma.

"It's too early to tell," says Fred, "but if anyone deserves the prize money, I think it's these two."

"Like, you guys aren't acting very impartial," says Shaggy. "Shouldn't we at least wait until —"

"Shhh!" Velma says again.

"Group #4," says Principal Hawthorne. The three ghosts walk onstage.

Turn the page.

"I've seen enough," Daphne says. "Let's give the prize to the Mystery Inc. gang and be done with it."

But before that can happen, the three ghosts walk to the judges' table. They pull masks off the heads of Fred, Velma, and Daphne, revealing three kids Scooby and Shaggy have never seen. Then they take off their own sheets, revealing the real Fred, Daphne, and Velma.

"Nice try with your witch distraction," the real Daphne says, "but we found your little projection device upstairs."

"Taking our places to rig the contest?" says Fred. "That's just dirty pool."

"Is this true?" Principal Hawthorne demands.

"Um," says the fake Shaggy. "Zoinks?"

As Principal Hawthorne escorts the fake gang off the stage, the real Fred, Daphne, and Velma take their seats next to Scooby and Shaggy.

"Like, I only have one question," says Shaggy. "Did you happen to see the treat table upstairs?"

THE END

To follow another path, turn to page 12.

"Well done, gang," the man says when he walks up to the picnic house. "Here's your share."

Velma immediately recognizes the figure handing out money to the four teens and their dog. "Principal Hawthorne!" she says under her breath.

"But that was just a trial run," Principal Hawthorne continues. He hands out five black robes to the teens, along with pointy black hats. "The real money is at the concert downtown tonight. At twenty dollars a head, their box office should offer a nice haul when all's said and done. Then I can finally get out of this cursed town."

"'Cursed town?'" whispers Shaggy from behind the wall. "Like, why do all our bad guys talk like that?"

Scooby just shrugs at his friend. The others seem to ignore him. Shaggy decides it's a step in the right direction. At least no one shushed him this time.

"The zip-lines are all in place," says Principal Hawthorne. "I'll see you five tonight."

Turn the page.

An hour later, a rather large crowd has gathered at a street blocked off downtown. Three elderly women are seated near the front gate, happy to stuff latecomers' admission fees into an already overstuffed till.

A band near the opposite end of the street is busy plugging in instruments and adjusting microphone stands on a temporary stage that's been set up for the night's celebration. As the lead singer taps on his microphone, it emits a high-pitched screech.

As if taking the feedback as a cue, five witches suddenly appear atop a nearby building. They soar down through the sky on cleverly disguised zip-lines, landing directly near the old women and their till.

One of the witches snags the money and rejoins the group. Then the five of them run past the barricades, jumping into the back of a pickup truck that speeds away into the night.

The elderly ladies at the front gate don't even have time to scream. All of the night's money is gone.

Back at the park, the five witches hop out of the back of the pickup truck, shedding their robes. Underneath, they're all still wearing Mystery Inc. costumes.

Principal Hawthorne steps out of the truck and smiles. "Excellent," he says. "Well done, my little witches."

"So what's our cut?" asks the fake Shaggy.

"Well, let's see," says Hawthorne. He walks over to the picnic house in the empty park and takes a seat at one of the tables. He places the cashbox on the table and begins to count out the money.

"You know," says fake Velma, "I've heard stories about stealing from the town of Salem."

"Huh?" says fake Daphne.

"Oh, yeah," says fake Velma. "They say that those who take from the town are destined to have their lives taken from them."

"They are correct," says a spooky voice from behind the picnic house's wall.

Turn to page 93.

"We dodged that bullet, huh, Scoobs?" says Shaggy as he and Scooby-Doo casually cross the street. With the sun already set, the two are happy to go anywhere witch-free. "Like, a pirate museum has to be the safest place in town. Plus, they might even have free eye patches!"

"Reah!" Scooby agrees. "Rye ratches!"

At the museum's front door, Shaggy pulls at the handle. It doesn't budge.

"Raybe rush?" says Scooby.

"Nah, Scoobs," says Shaggy. "I'll try to push."

"Rat's rhat ri said," says Scooby-Doo.

"You're not making any sense, old buddy," Shaggy says as he pushes the door. It still doesn't open.

"Ruh-roh," says Scooby. He points to the sign in the nearby window.

"Ah, bummer," says Shaggy, reading the sign. "It's closed." He looks at his reflection in the window. He blinks, and another figure appears in the reflection as well.

Standing there behind him is a dark figure wrapped in black robes. On her head is a pointy black hat. Its large brim nearly hides her long, oddly shaped nose.

"A-a-a-a —" Shaggy starts to say.

"Rich!" Scooby-Doo shouts.

Shaggy and Scooby take off running. Clouds of dust shoot out from under their feet as they sprint away from the pirate museum.

"Over here!" shouts a voice from a nearby alley.

Shaggy stops in his tracks. There in the alleyway are Fred, Velma, and Daphne. They're hard to make out because they're standing in the shadows, but Shaggy is pretty sure it's them.

"Guys?" Shaggy says. He and Scooby-Doo abruptly change course and head into the dark space between buildings.

It's not until they're standing five feet away from the rest of the gang that Shaggy sees his friends are not alone. There next to Fred, Daphne, and Velma stand another Scooby-Doo and another Shaggy!

Turn the page.

"Like, holy double standard!" Shaggy says. He and Scooby-Doo stare at their duplicates.

"Don't you guys remember us?" asks the fake Shaggy. "Like, from the costume contest."

"Oh, yeah," says Shaggy. His voice gets calmer. "I forgot about you guys. What's shaking?"

"Your dog," says the fake Shaggy.

Shaggy looks over at Scooby-Doo and sees that his good buddy is indeed shivering more than usual. "It's OK, pal," says Shaggy. "These are the good guys."

"Roh," says Scooby. "Rokay." He wipes a bead of sweat from his forehead with his paw.

"So what brings you guys out to a creepy locale like this?" Shaggy asks.

"Same as you, I guess," says the fake Fred. "We're hunting witches."

Turn to page 58.

"The door isn't budging," says Shaggy. "Like, we're gonna have to find another way out."

Scooby and Shaggy walk across the locker room toward the boarded-up door. "This one looks like it hasn't been opened for decades," Shaggy says.

Suddenly, there's a thump, and all the boards fall to the ground. The door opens slowly toward the locker room.

Scooby-Doo and Shaggy look at each other. The pals sprint toward the nearby lockers.

By the time the boarded-up door has fully opened, Scooby and Shaggy are each safely inside of one of the dusty lockers.

"No, I left it in here," a young teenager with jet-black hair says, walking into the room.

"Well, hurry up!" says a voice from the other side of the door. "We've got to get in our vampire costumes."

"Here it is," says the boy. He picks up a cell phone resting on the floor by one of the lockers.

Shaggy watches through the slats on his locker, wondering how he missed that obvious clue.

The teen takes the phone and walks out of the room. The door starts to shut behind him.

Scooby and Shaggy burst out of their lockers. They slip through just before it closes.

"Like, I don't know how they got that old door to open, but I'm glad we didn't try and figure it out ourselves," Shaggy says.

The two look around. They're in a storage closet. There's no sign of the black-haired boy or whoever he was talking to. But in the corner is a pile of witch costumes and what looks like a pulley system of some kind.

"Rich rostumes!" says Scooby.

"You got that right, buddy," says Shaggy. "Guess us two fearless detectives figured out yet another caper all by our lonesome."

Suddenly, one of the pulleys falls off a shelf, causing a loud thud. Scooby-Doo and Shaggy run to the door of the janitor's closet, but it's locked.

Turn the page.

"Oh, man," says Shaggy. "Like, any idea how to deduce our way out of this mess?"

Scooby just shrugs.

"Those phony witches are probably onstage right now," says Shaggy. "They've scared away all the other competitors so they could win the prize money in those cheap vampire suits."

"Reah," Scooby agrees.

"Just our luck — we solve a case, and we're not around to let anybody know," Shaggy says. He and Scooby put their backs to the door and slide down to the cool concrete underneath them.

"Reah," Scooby says again.

Suddenly, the door opens behind them. Scooby and Shaggy fall backward, their heads thumping on the hard floor.

They can barely see the man standing above them. Thanks to the light on the ceiling, he just looks like a large, dark shadow with crazy, wild hair.

Turn to page 62.

By the time Scooby-Doo and Shaggy find their way from the treat table to the front of the school, Velma, Fred, and Daphne are about to leave.

"There you guys are!" says Daphne. "Come on!"

"Like, where are we going?" asks Shaggy as he piles into the back of the Mystery Machine.

"After those three witches," says Fred, putting his key into the ignition.

The Mystery Machine's engine hums as Fred pulls out slowly. He follows a wide brown car that looks like it belongs in the 1970s.

"What three witches?" Shaggy asks.

"The ones from the costume contest," says Velma. "Principal Hawthorne checked all the students' bags and pockets, but he didn't look in the witches' hats."

"For dandruff?" Shaggy is confused.

"For the prize money," says Daphne.

"Oh," says Shaggy. "That makes way more sense."

Turn the page.

The brown car continues past downtown Salem. Eventually it turns off on a dimly lit road.

Fred follows the vehicle, happy that the moon has come out from behind the clouds. It helps him see the road much better than the Mystery Machine's dull headlights alone.

A few moments later, the brown car turns down a short private lane. It slows to a stop in front of a small row house.

Fred parks the Mystery Machine on the street nearby. He and the rest of the gang duck down as the three witches exit their car and file into the house, one by one.

Fred pops his head up and peers out the window. "OK," he says. "Coast is clear."

The Mystery Inc. gang exits the van and quickly makes their way to the front of the house. Daphne peers in the house's front window while the rest of the gang ducks against the house to avoid being seen. She can see the three witches as they take a seat on their couch.

"Well, we got away with it," says the witch on the left.

Daphne and Fred look at each other. That's all the evidence they need.

Fred stands up and hurries to the front door. He throws it open with the rest of the Mystery Inc. gang close behind him.

"Aha!" Fred hollers.

"Like, he's really got to work on his dramatic lines," says Shaggy. "It should have been something snappy like, 'It's trick-or-treat time, and we're all out of treats!'"

Scooby-Doo just shakes his head.

"No?" says Shaggy. "I thought it was snappy."

"Looks like you didn't get away with it after all," Velma says to the three witches.

"Oh, dear," says the witch on the left. "How did you know?"

"It was the only logical explanation," says Velma.

Turn to page 65.

"Sure," says Shaggy. "Us too. Just two brave witch hunters out to catch the bad guys."

"We should probably compare notes," says the fake Velma. She pulls out a notebook from her pocket. "We need to find out who those witches are — and why they're hanging around Salem — before they ruin the costume contest."

"Ha!" says Shaggy. "You guys *are* new at this."

"Reah!" says Scooby-Doo.

"Trust us, when you've been at this mystery game as long as me and my pal Scoobs here, you don't have to write anything down," says Shaggy. "I've got a mind like a steel . . . a steel . . ."

"A steel what?" asks the fake Daphne.

"Trap!" Shaggy hollers, pointing behind the fake Mystery Inc. There, hovering in the shadows, are the three witches the gang spotted earlier.

"Like, run for it!" Shaggy yells.

Scooby-Doo and Shaggy run out of the alley so quickly that they forget the most important rule of running away — look where you're going!

Shaggy accidentally steps on Scooby's tail, tripping him. Scooby slips and slams into a pile of trash bags lining one of the alleyway walls. The bags fall on top of him, one by one.

If that isn't bad enough, a black cat has been sleeping on one of the bags. It awakens with a start and leaps into the air. The cat falls to the ground, one of the witches' robes stuck to its claws.

"You did it!" shouts fake Fred as he walks over to the pile of garbage bags that have pinned Scooby and Shaggy to the alleyway floor.

With the help of the fake Mystery Inc. gang, Scooby and Shaggy manage to dig their way out from under the pile of garbage. Shaggy looks over to the fake Velma, who is holding an empty black robe in her hands.

"How did you guys figure it out?" she asks.

"Like, figure what out?" asks Shaggy.

"That the witches were just remote-controlled drones outfitted to look like your average storybook sorceresses," says the fake Velma.

Turn the page.

Velma pulls the robe off of the drone, revealing a small metal flying machine with four propellers.

"Hey! You broke my —" a voice shouts from the end of the alleyway.

The fake gang and the real Scooby-Doo and Shaggy all turn to see Principal Hawthorne. He is standing in the alleyway holding a remote control.

"I mean, you broke that . . . oh. Shoot," the principal says.

"Something you want to tell us?" asks Fake Fred.

"Fine. You got me," the principal says. "I was trying to scare people off. The school doesn't have the funds for the prize money. We spent it on —"

"Let me guess," says fake Velma. "Drones?"

"You can't prove that," Principal Hawthorne says. "I tell you, I would have gotten away with it too if it hadn't been for you meddling kids, and . . ."

Principal Hawthorne looks at Shaggy and Scooby. Then he looks at the fake Mystery Incorporated gang. "And . . . well, you other . . . meddling kids."

THE END

To follow another path, turn to page 12.

Meanwhile, in the auditorium, Fred, Velma, and Daphne have stalled as long as possible. They found nothing suspicious upstairs. When they returned to the auditorium, it was nearly empty.

A few minutes ago, however, three teens dressed as vampires sat back down in their seats. The winner of the costume contest seems clear.

But the gang still tries to stall. The vampires look like they spent five minutes on their costumes. And something seems off about their smiles.

"We should wait until Scooby and Shaggy get back," says Velma. "We need all our judges to vote."

"We've been waiting for nearly an hour," says Principal Hawthorne. "Let's just get this over with."

"OK," says Fred, sighing. "The winner of the Third Annual Salem High Costume Contest is —"

"Nobody!" shouts Shaggy, slamming the door open. He strikes a dramatic pose next to Scooby. With them is a man with crazy brown hair carrying a mop. The nametag on his chest reads, *Melvin, School Janitor.*

"Where have you been?" Velma asks.

"We got stuck in the janitor's closet," Shaggy says. "Melvin let us out."

Shaggy strolls triumphantly into the room and up to the seated vampires. "We saw this guy —" he says as he pulls the first vampire's mask off.

Underneath is a blond teenage girl.

"Whoops," Shaggy says. "I mean, this guy —"

He pulls off the second vampire's mask. It's another young woman, this one with dark braids.

"OK, so it's this guy!" Shaggy says, pulling off the third vampire's mask.

The third time is a charm. Underneath is the black-haired boy from the locker room.

"Phew!" Shaggy says. "I was running out of vampires."

Then Shaggy composes himself, realizing he's still addressing the room. "We saw this guy in the locker room. He and his group here posed as those witches to scare away the competition."

Turn the page.

"Is this true, Erik?" asks Principal Hawthorne.

"Yes, it's true," the boy mutters.

"The dynamic duo strikes again!" Shaggy says.

Principal Hawthorne turns to the three vampires. "I'll have to call your parents to discuss your punishment," he says. "This is such a shame."

"That the contest is ruined?" asks Velma.

"Well, yes," says Principal Hawthorne, "but also, part of the costume prize was a visit to our treat table backstage. I'm afraid we have much too much candy and donuts for just you judges."

"That was the treat table?" says Shaggy. "I thought those were the appetizers. I'm starved."

"We'll see ourselves out," says Daphne, slinking away from the astonished principal.

"Wait, what?" says Principal Hawthorne. "There are at least five dozen donuts alone . . ."

But the gang has already made their getaway.

THE END

To follow another path, turn to page 12.

The sound of sirens fills the air. Velma turns to look out the still-open door. Two squad cars pull up on either side of the Mystery Machine. An officer exits the driver's side of each police car, and they both walk up to the house's front door.

Velma points to the witches. "There they are!" But the police officer handcuffs Velma instead.

"Hey, what are you doing?" Fred asks as the second officer fits him with a pair of handcuffs.

"Oh, my," says the witch in the center of the couch. She takes off her hat and pointy nose, revealing the face of a woman at least 80 years old.

"I don't understand," says Daphne as the police officers place her in handcuffs as well. "You're . . . you're not high school students at all."

"I thought you said you knew our secret," says the witch on the right. She takes off her nose and hat, appearing about the same age as her friend.

As Shaggy and Scooby-Doo are placed in handcuffs, the final witch takes off her nose and hat. She seems to be the oldest of the bunch.

Turn the page.

"I know we shouldn't have, because it's just for students, but we just love a good costume party," she says. "So we snuck in. I hope we weren't a bother."

"No bother at all, ma'am," says the first police officer. "It's these kids that committed the real crime, stealing that prize money."

"What?" says Daphne. "We didn't steal a thing!"

"Save it for downtown," the second police officer says. He takes Daphne's arm and leads her to his squad car. "Somebody snapped a picture that clearly shows you kids grabbing that money."

"Oh, dear," says the oldest woman as she watches the cops load the members of Mystery Inc. into their squad cars.

The gang are in their jail cell a good hour before Principal Hawthorne arrives. "This way, sir," says one of the officers to him. They walk to the cell, and the officer unlocks the door.

"Well, you're cleared," says Principal Hawthorne.

"We are?" asks Daphne.

"Turns out it was the other Mystery Inc. that did it — the fake bunch," says Hawthorne. "They stole the money and then hid it under one of the chairs in the auditorium. The janitor saw them retrieving it, but he wasn't quick enough to stop them."

"That's terrible!" Velma exclaims.

"You're free to go," says Principal Hawthorne. "But do me a favor and stay out of Salem. We can't afford your type of trouble."

Dejected, the gang files out of the cell, out of the jail, and into the Mystery Machine. None of them says a word as they drive out of Salem, thinking of the three innocent old witches they put on trial on their own.

THE END

To follow another path, turn to page 12.

"That looks like the only sign of civilization," says Velma, pointing to the gas station.

"I think you're right," Fred agrees.

The Mystery Inc. gang walks toward the station. The place looks dark and empty. The only sign of life is a red neon light that reads *OPEN* in its window.

Fred walks up to the door first and tries it. It's a bit stuck, but he manages to pull it open. "Hello?" he says.

"Well, hi!" says a man popping up from behind the dark counter.

Velma takes a step back in surprise. Fred clenches his jaw. Daphne lets out a gasp. Scooby-Doo and Shaggy simply fall down, fainting in fear.

"Didn't mean to startle you," says the man.

When he smiles, the gang realizes just how many teeth he is missing — it's a lot.

"How can I help you?" the man asks.

"Do you happen to have a phone?" asks Velma. The gang all agreed to leave theirs in the van earlier in the day. They didn't want them to ring while they were judging the costume contest.

"Yes, I do, ma'am," says the man, leaning over the counter. The neon light in the window illuminates him more clearly now. His eyebrows seem to connect, making an oddly jagged line on his forehead. Thin wisps of blond hair poke down from a well-loved baseball cap. "It's down that hall, in the stock room."

Velma thanks him, and with Daphne by her side, attempts to navigate the dark hallway in the back of the store. Scooby-Doo and Shaggy follow her, with Fred taking up the rear. They all find the stock room and head inside.

Velma picks up the phone that's sitting on a desk. There's no dial tone. "I think the phone's dead," she says.

"Let me take a look," says Fred. He walks over toward her and hears a faint click behind him.

Turn to page 75.

Daphne can't help but shiver as she leads the way into the dark room beneath the bleachers. The room smells of dust and old books. And as it turns out, it's filled with both.

Velma trips over a pile of old textbooks stacked haphazardly near her feet. "My glasses!" she says as she falls.

The other members of Mystery Inc. don't answer — mainly because Daphne is currently screaming so loudly that it drowns out Velma's cries for help.

"Something touched my face!" Daphne screams. "It's . . . it's on me!"

While he can't see her, Fred reaches toward the sound of Daphne's voice. His fingers touch her face, but also a metal cord of some kind. He pulls it. A single lightbulb comes to brilliant life.

Turn the page.

"It was just the chain to the light," Fred says.

"I gathered that, Fred," Daphne says. "Thanks."

"Could somebody help me find my glasses?" says Velma from the ground nearby.

Daphne hands Velma her frames — complete with new additions to her scratched lenses collection — while Fred looks around the room. There are piles of dusty old textbooks and library books that look decades past their checkout dates. There are also rows upon rows of folding chairs, tattered blue gym mats, and a shadowy corner where something — or someone — is standing.

"Um . . . um . . . guys?" Fred manages to say.

"H-hello?" Daphne says to the shadowy figure in the corner. To her, it looks like more than one person.

With her glasses on, Velma's eyesight is a little better than Fred's and Daphne's. She walks over to the dark corner and reaches out toward the shadowy figure.

Turn to page 79.

Scooby-Doo walks over to the painting of the witch and looks at it closely. Shaggy joins the Great Dane, standing right in front of the painting.

"Her eyes are so lifelike," Shaggy said.

Just then, the painting blinks.

"Ri'll say!" Scooby says, jolting backward.

"Zoinks!" says Shaggy. "Like, I think that painting is alive."

Suddenly, the eyes disappear altogether, leaving two small oval holes. It takes the pair a good four minutes before they figure out what happened.

"Like, somebody was back there!" Shaggy says.

Scooby-Doo is already way ahead of his human friend. He's pulling and prying at the frame with his front paws.

"I don't know if that's such a good —" Shaggy starts to say.

Scooby falls to the ground. The painting is on a pair of hinges and has opened like a door.

Turn the page.

"Like, I'm not going in there," says Shaggy, looking into a dark tunnel set into the wall behind the painting.

"Me reither!" agrees Scooby-Doo.

"Like, it's totally spooky," says Shaggy. "I can't imagine ever being dumb enough to go in there willing —"

At that very second, a plate of donuts falls off the table. Scooby-Doo and Shaggy jump into the air and take off into the tunnel to escape whatever made the loud sound. The painting closes behind them.

Shaggy and Scooby don't regain their senses until they're halfway down the tunnel.

"Oh man, Scoob," says Shaggy. "Like, what did we just do?"

Scooby-Doo shakes his head, but Shaggy can't see him. The tunnel is too dark, and his eyes have yet to adjust.

Turn to page 83.

The gang looks toward the door of the stock room. It's been shut behind them. Fred tries the handle. It's locked.

"I'm sorry, but you all need to stay put," the gas station attendant says from the other side. "You're going to keep me safe this year."

"What are you talking about?" asks Daphne, her voice full of panic.

"The witches," says the man. "They like young kids. You five will do just fine. That way they'll leave me alone."

"Zoinks!" says Shaggy. "Like, when they asked me what I wanted to do when I grow up, I always said something like doctor or ninja. Witch sacrifice was never even on the list."

"There's got to be some way out of here," says Velma. "Look around the room for an exit."

"Here!" says Fred from the far side of the stock room. "Over here, guys!"

In front of Fred is a large metal garage door. "Give me a hand," he says.

Turn the page.

Fred and Shaggy bend down and try to lift the metal gate. It doesn't budge. Velma and Daphne add their strength. Even Scooby-Doo tries to lift it. It still doesn't move.

"I can't believe this," says Velma. "Witches — real witches, I mean. This can't be happening."

Just then, the door begins to rattle as if someone is pounding on it from the outside. Then the gang hears the familiar sound of cackling. It's the witches.

"Like, if they're not real, then they're certainly doing a good job of figmenting our imaginations," says Shaggy.

The gate continues to shake. Then there's a clicking noise. The metal garage door slowly begins to rise.

"Well," says Shaggy, "this is it. Man, I hate to become witch food on an empty stomach."

The gate continues to rise until the gang sees what's standing on the other side. In front of them are the three witches — but that's not all.

There are also several vampires, a few ghosts, some goblins, the gas station attendant, and one smiling Principal Hawthorne. "Got ya!" he says.

"Like, you do?" says Shaggy.

"Happy Halloween!" the group yells at once.

"Wait, this was all a prank?" asks Fred, still a little confused.

"Well, when we invited Mystery Inc. to town, we figured we had to give you guys a proper mystery," says Principal Hawthorne. "We've been working on this gag for months. Just rigging the wire system to make the witches look authentic took a good three weeks."

"Ha!" says Shaggy, turning to his friends. "They sure got you guys! You should have seen the look on your —"

"Mr. Shaggy," says one of the witches, touching Shaggy on the shoulder.

Shaggy doesn't answer, though. He's a bit too busy diving beneath a stockroom table to hide.

THE END

To follow another path, turn to page 12.

"It's just a mannequin, you guys," Velma says, lifting the dark figure out of the shadows. "There are three of them back here."

"And they're all dressed like witches," says Daphne as Velma walks one over to her.

"Just like the ones who interrupted the costume contest," says Fred.

"And look at this," says Velma. She hands Fred a spool of clear fishing line. "Here's how our mystery man made them defy gravity. Probably rigged up to the stage's winch system. Like when they make actors seem to fly in a production of *Peter Pan* or something."

"But these actors are much lighter, so they can use the fishing line," says Fred, "and it'll look like they're really flying on their broomsticks."

"Looked real enough to me," Daphne mutters.

"Hey, ya' bunch of Nancy Drews," calls the janitor from the doorway, "you about done in my closet yet?"

Turn the page.

A few moments later, Fred and Daphne walk back into the auditorium.

"Like, are we glad to see you guys," says Shaggy. "We thought you'd been cooked up in witch's brew or something."

"There's definitely something cooking," says Fred. "But it's not our gooses."

"Oh, man, Scoobs," Shaggy says. "You know what that means. Like, Fred's got another foolproof plan. Those usually end with us running through way too many doorways with some monster hot on our heels."

"Ruh-roh," says Scooby.

"Hey," says Shaggy. "Where's Velma, anyway?"

Before Fred can answer, Principal Hawthorne steps up to the microphone on the stage. He taps on it and then begins to speak.

"Attention, students," Principal Hawthorne says. "In light of the recent . . . commotion . . . this year's Halloween costume contest is now cancelled. Please —"

Just then, the three witches burst out from behind the curtains. Principal Hawthorne is so surprised by their arrival that he knocks over the microphone stand.

Suddenly, all three witches dive toward the stage. They collide with the principal, who falls back into the empty judges' table.

"This isn't possible!" the principal shouts.

"And why is that?" asks Daphne.

While Scooby-Doo and Shaggy are busy hiding under the first row of seats, Daphne doesn't appear the least bit afraid. She walks over to Principal Hawthorne as the three witches fall onto the stage, as limp as the mannequins they are.

Just then Velma walks out from behind the curtains. "Boy, those controls are fun to work," she says. "I feel like I'm on Broadway!"

"Wait," says Principal Hawthorne from his position on the floor by the judges' table. "It was . . . you . . ."

Turn the page.

"Well, you did provide the inspiration," says Velma. "We just had to reattach your witches."

"No," says Hawthorne, "wait . . . how?"

"According to the school janitor, only two people have keys to the bleacher storage space," says Daphne. "You're one, and the janitor is the other. And he was too busy cleaning up the chemistry room to worry about scaring people away from the contest."

"It's just . . . it's just so much work," says Principal Hawthorne. "The school board won't even pay overtime, and these kids, they trash the place and . . ."

"Save it for your own witch trial," says Velma. She smiles at the rest of the Mystery Inc. gang, and they all smile back. Another mystery solved!

THE END

To follow another path, turn to page 12.

Shaggy and Scooby have no choice but to walk deeper into the mysterious tunnel.

"You know, now that I think about it," says Shaggy, "I bet whoever snagged that prize money made off with it down this tunnel."

"Reah," Scooby agrees.

"But boy, do I not want to meet them," says Shaggy.

"Reah," Scooby says again. The two keep moving further down the dark tunnel.

"Any idea why we're still walking then?" asks Shaggy.

"Ru-uh," says Scooby-Doo, shaking his head.

Just then, a light turns on, causing Shaggy and Scooby to shield their eyes. When their eyes adjust, they realize they've walked into a new room altogether.

The tunnel is behind them now. They enter a room decorated with framed portraits. In the center of the odd room sits a round table with a letter on top.

Turn to page 85.

Shaggy walks over to the table and picks up the letter. The framed portraits stare down at him. They're all of young women and look to be as old as the painting backstage.

"Like, 'To whom it may concern,'" reads Shaggy. "'I have been accused by the town of Salem, Massachusetts, of being a witch. While I deny these accusations, if the town finds me guilty, know that I will haunt it from the afterlife, along with the rest of the falsely accused. I will steal the riches from those who stole my life. Signed, Eleanor Paige.'"

Shaggy looks back in the envelope. It contains five hundred dollars — it's the prize money.

Shaggy and Scooby look at each other. Without saying a word, the pair scampers back through the tunnel, through the auditorium, and out of the school as fast as their legs can carry them.

When Fred, Velma, and Daphne return to the Mystery Machine, it takes them a good fifteen minutes to convince Shaggy and Scooby to unlock the van. Even then, the pair stays hidden under their blanket until the gang is well out of Salem.

THE END

To follow another path, turn to page 12.

Realizing their friends are no longer at their side, Scooby-Doo and Shaggy finally come to a stop and turn around.

"Like, guys!" calls Shaggy. "I may not be the sharpest knife in the drawer, but I know one thing — never stop when witches are chasing you. I mean, don't you know about Hansel and Gretel?"

"They're gone," says Daphne as she walks over to Scooby and Shaggy.

"Well, I'm not stopping for anyone," says Shaggy. He and Scooby-Doo turn toward the rickety covered bridge down the road and start walking.

"We should head back to town," says Velma.

"Ro ray!" says Scooby-Doo.

"Yeah," says Shaggy, "I'm with the dog. No way! Town equals witches. I'm gonna keep walking until I hit Boston."

Fred, Daphne, and Velma exchange a glance. They shrug and then follow their friends.

"OK," says Shaggy as he walks inside the covered wooden bridge. "I may not be the sharpest knife in the drawer, but I know one thing."

"I think that's two things," says Fred.

Shaggy ignores him. "I know you should never listen to the guy that's not the sharpest knife in the drawer," he says.

Shaggy's eyes dart around at the inside of the covered bridge. There are strange markings in red paint all over the walls and ceiling. At least, Shaggy hopes they were made in red paint.

"Whoa," says Daphne as she walks into the bridge. "What's all this stuff?"

"Don't ask me," says Velma, feeling everyone's eyes on her. "This isn't the sort of thing you can read about at your local library."

Just then, a cackling sound echoes through the bridge.

"This isn't a laughing matter, Scoobs," says Shaggy. "Like, can't you see this is serious?"

"Rasn't me," Scooby-Doo says.

Turn the page.

The cackling gets louder.

"Like, gulp," Shaggy says. "Please tell me that's you, Daph?"

"N-n-no," Daphne stutters. "Not me."

The high-pitched cackling gets louder still.

"Don't look at me," says Fred.

"Or me," says Velma.

"Oh, man," say Shaggy as the cackling continues to echo throughout the covered bridge. "Like, I really hope it's me then."

Shaggy looks to the far end of the bridge and sees two shadowy figures hovering in the moonlit air. He looks back the way they came and sees a third witch slowly floating toward them. Then he looks straight ahead and sees a small hole in the covered bridge's wall. It's large enough to fit a person about his size.

Turn to page 96.

"C'mon, ya dawdlers," says the now-angry janitor. "Get away from there. That's not for snoopy kids."

"Wrong dog," says Daphne.

"What'd you say?" the janitor snaps.

"Never mind," says Velma. "We were just leaving."

"You bet you were," says the janitor, literally shooing them away with his mop.

Three wet backsides and one jog down the stairs later, and Mystery Inc. is still nowhere closer to solving the mystery than when they started. Fred, Daphne, and Velma walk back into the auditorium to find it completely empty.

"Guess everyone cleared out," says Velma.

"Not everyone," comes a voice from seemingly nowhere.

Turn the page.

"Shaggy, is that you?" Fred says, recognizing the voice.

"That depends," says Shaggy's voice from out of thin air. "You three aren't witches in disguise, are you?"

"Um, no," says Velma. "Although we've been called worse."

Suddenly, Shaggy and Scooby-Doo pop up from beneath a row of seats in the middle of the auditorium. "Like, hey guys," says Shaggy. Scooby-Doo waves.

"Did we miss anything?" asks Velma.

"Like, just a return visit from the twisted sisters," says Shaggy. "The audience pretty much split when those three came back and started buzzing overhead again. But me and Scoobs, we stayed put. You know, to make sure you guys were safe."

"Reah!" says Scooby.

"Wow," says Velma, sounding underwhelmed. "Um, thanks?"

"No problem," says Shaggy as he and Scooby-Doo stroll over toward their friends. "Like, what are friends for?"

"Rey! Randy!" Scooby-Doo says, examining the bottom of his front paw.

"What's that?" says Fred. He walks over to his canine friend and tugs at Scooby's paw. He holds up a small locket, blackened, as if it were in a fire. "That's not candy, buddy. Looks like you stepped on somebody's necklace."

Fred opens the locket. It has not just one, but four places for pictures inside it. Only three are in use, though, fit with tiny black-and-white photographs, each of a different young woman.

"Jinkies," says Velma. "Those pictures look ancient."

Turn to page 98.

"You have stolen from Salem," says a voice from behind the picnic house's wall. A woman in a witch outfit steps out into the dim light of the evening. "And now Salem will steal from you!"

Principal Hawthorne and the fake gang spring to their feet. They race toward the parked pickup, only to see two more witches standing in its bed.

The phony gang turns around and races toward the street. There seem to be no witches blocking the path now. But then they see the flashing lights.

A police car pulls up in front of the principal and his fake gang. Without giving it a second thought, they leap into the back of the car. The police officer closes the door as the witches draw closer.

The first witch takes off her mask. It's the real Velma. The others do the same. One by one the witches reveal themselves as the true Mystery Inc.

As the police car pulls away toward the station, Principal Hawthorne and his fake Mystery Inc. gang have no choice but to watch as the real Mystery Inc. waves them a happy farewell.

THE END

To follow another path, turn to page 12.

Scooby-Doo shrugs and goes back to eating. Shaggy is way ahead of him, working now on the plate of donuts.

"No, just some kid and his dog," comes a muffled voice behind the painting. "No, they don't suspect a thing. I'll just wait here until they leave and then meet you out front."

"Well, I'm stuffed," says Shaggy, looking over to his best buddy.

"Reah," Scooby says. "Re too!"

The two stretch, grab a few donuts for the walk, and exit the room, heading back onto the stage and then into the auditorium.

"Like, hey, gang," says Shaggy, as he sees Velma, Fred, and Daphne talking to a group of poorly costumed ghosts. "Any luck?"

"Not on our end," says Fred.

Just then a man wearing a janitor's uniform walks out from backstage and makes his way into the auditorium. He pauses for a second, then looks around and leaves the room.

Shaggy watches him go and then sees the fake Mystery Inc. get up out of their chairs and head toward the door as well. The principal and the city councilwoman stop the group as they're about to leave and ask them to empty their pockets. They've been doing the same thing to any student who leaves the auditorium. The prize money is still unaccounted for.

"Well, the treat table is . . . mostly intact," says Shaggy. "But there was this crazy sneezing painting, and I think somebody left their radio on back there."

"Radio?" asks Daphne.

"Yeah, I could hear a voice as I was eating all . . . I mean taking inventory of the donuts," Shaggy says. "Something about meeting out front. About some kid and a dog not suspecting anything. Weird nonsense like that."

Turn to page 103.

"Like, coward overboard!" Shaggy yells. He runs straight ahead and leaps through the hole in the covered bridge's wall.

A few seconds later, Shaggy hits the water below with a splash that seems too big for someone so skinny. He looks up at the bridge just in time to see Scooby-Doo leap toward him, followed by Velma, Daphne, and then Fred.

With his friends behind him, Shaggy swims faster than he has ever swum in his life. It's a good ten minutes before he checks to make sure his friends are still with him — fortunately, they are.

"Are they — *PANT!* — are they following us?" Shaggy manages to ask.

"I don't see anyone," says Fred.

"There's a bank up ahead," says Velma.

The gang swims toward the beach and climbs out of the cold, murky water. Scooby-Doo shakes off, giving the rest of the gang a second chance at being drenched in river water.

The gang walks up the shore toward the woods beyond.

"Come on," says Velma. "There's a light up ahead."

Reluctantly, Shaggy and Scooby-Doo follow Velma. Fred and Daphne follow too. The gang walks through the woods, pushing shrubs and tall weeds out of their way. The light gets brighter as they get closer to it. Soon, they reach a clearing.

Fred leads the way out of the forest and onto the road surrounding it. "Oh," he says, when he sees where the light is coming from. "Oh, boy."

The light is originating from the Mystery Machine. The gang's van is mysteriously parked by the side of the road — nowhere close to the school parking lot where they left it.

With their nerves on edge, the Mystery Inc. gang piles inside the empty vehicle. Fred turns the key in the ignition. They decide to drive as far away from Salem as they can make it on a single tank of gas.

As they sit silently, thinking of the night's events, none of them notice the frayed broom resting on the floor in the back of the van . . .

THE END

To follow another path, turn to page 12.

With the locket in hand, the gang heads back to their familiar van.

"So what's the plan, oh fearless leader?" Shaggy asks, looking at Fred.

"We get that locket looked at," says Velma. "You were talking to me, right?" she says. "I just assumed you were talking to me."

"OK, let's go with that," says Fred. "It's as good a lead as any."

The gang piles into the Mystery Machine, and Fred drives them toward downtown Salem. When he sees a sign for the Salem Witch Museum, he pulls into the parking lot.

Velma, Daphne, and Fred leap out of the van and quickly make their way to the front door of the museum. Shaggy and Scooby are a bit slower. They make it to the front door but at a pace that would make a sloth impatient.

"Closed," says Velma.

"Someone's coming!" says Daphne. "Look!"

Turn to page 100.

As the gang watches, the doors slowly open. A figure appears. It's an old woman, probably around 90. She doesn't greet the gang with a hello or a smile or any other gesture. She simply looks into Daphne's eyes and says, "What is in your hand?"

"We were hoping you could tell us," says Daphne. She hands the locket to the old woman.

The woman gasps. "You need to get rid of this right now," she says. She hands the locket back and turns around to go back inside the museum.

"Why, what is it?" asks Daphne.

The old woman pauses. Then she turns back to face Daphne. "I had that locket when I was a girl," she says. "It calls them, the ones who were burned at the stake."

"Burned at the stake," Velma repeats. "Like during the Witch Trials?"

"Exactly," says the old woman. "Wherever that locket goes, they go. They are in endless torment from the flames that did them in."

"So what do we do with it?" Daphne asks.

The old woman doesn't answer. Her eyes focus on something in the distance, and her expression changes from surprise to one of outright terror. Suddenly she slams the museum doors shut and locks them from the inside.

"Like, what spooked her?" asks Shaggy.

"Riches!" says Scooby-Doo.

"Now that doesn't make any sense, old buddy," says Shaggy. "Why would money scare anyone?"

"Riches!" Scooby says again, this time pointing behind Shaggy. The lanky teen turns to see the three witches flying directly toward them.

"Like, consider me spooked," Shaggy says as he and the gang run for their lives.

The Mystery Inc. gang runs past the museum and down an old, winding road. They don't dare look behind them. They can hear the witches cackling. They keep running until the road dead ends at a cul-de-sac.

Fred points to a nearby footpath cutting through the trees. "This way!" he shouts.

Turn the page.

Daphne, Velma, Shaggy, and Scooby follow his lead. They run through the woods, dodging trees until the path dead ends at a sharp ravine.

Velma looks over the cliff. The gang turns and sees the witches flying directly at them.

"Give me that!" Velma yells as she snatches the locket from Daphne. She throws it over the cliff, and it splashes into a lake below.

The witches stop in their tracks and hover in front of Mystery Inc. Then they close their eyes and smile. They look relieved.

"Water," one says as the three fade away into thin air.

The gang looks around for any trace of the flying women. They look down at the water. None of them says anything, but two words echo from the base of the ravine.

"At last," the voice says, and then it too fades into the night air.

THE END

To follow another path, turn to page 12.

"Shaggy, that was no radio!" says Velma.

Fred and Daphne are already ahead of her. They're moving toward the auditorium's exit.

"Hold up a minute, gang," says Principal Hawthorne. "I need you to empty your pockets."

"But we need to get out front, right this second!" says Velma. "It's urgent."

"Everyone's a suspect here," says Principal Hawthorne, "as much as I hate to say it."

As Velma removes a wallet and a miniature flashlight from her pockets, a faint sound of music begins to play.

"Excuse me, Larry," Councilwoman Spindle says, removing a phone from her purse. "I need to step outside and take this."

"By all means," says Principal Hawthorne. He turns his attention to the contents of Daphne's purse.

Principal Hawthorne opens and closes Daphne's makeup compact, as if it could possibly contain the missing five hundred dollars.

Turn the page.

Velma can't take any more. "I'll meet you out there," she says, hurrying out the door. Daphne is soon hot on her heels.

Across the parking lot, a car's lights turn on. It pulls out of its parking space and drives past Velma and Daphne on its way out of the lot. Through its windows, Velma sees the fake Mystery Inc.

"They're getting away!" she says.

"Maybe not," says Fred as he hurries out of the door toward the girls. "Look over there!" He points near the corner of the school where the janitor is talking to a shadowy figure.

"Hold it right there!" says Fred.

The figure turns around and steps into the light. It's Councilwoman Spindle. "What's the problem, kids?" she asks.

"That envelope is the problem," says Daphne. "The one the janitor just handed to you."

Just then, Scooby-Doo and Shaggy make it outside. Curious, Scooby moves toward the councilwoman. She doesn't see him and takes a step back, tripping over the Great Dane.

The contents of the envelope go flying through the air — five hundred dollars exactly.

The councilwoman sighs from her position on the sidewalk. "Take the money. It's never been about a few measly dollars," she says. "Halloween is the problem. So many tourists . . ."

"So much cleanup," says the janitor.

"So much traffic," the councilwoman finishes. "I just wanted to shut it down. Make any little dent in this awful holiday that I can."

"Like, I know she explained the plot," says Shaggy, "but I still have no idea what's going on."

Velma is about to explain, but Shaggy and Scooby-Doo are already halfway back to the school's front door by then.

"Best way to figure it out is more research," Shaggy says. "Back to the treat table, Scoobs!"

Velma smiles, then steels herself as she turns back to the councilwoman and the janitor. She finds it best to look serious — at least until the police arrive.

THE END

To follow another path, turn to page 12.

AUTHOR

The author of the Amazon best-selling hardcover *Batman: A Visual History*, Matthew K. Manning has contributed to many comic books, including *Beware the Batman*, *Spider-Man Unlimited*, *Pirates of the Caribbean: Six Sea Shanties*, *Justice League Adventures*, *Looney Tunes*, and *Scooby-Doo, Where Are You?* When not writing comics themselves, Manning often authors books about comics, as well as a series of young reader books starring Superman, Batman, and the Flash for Capstone. He currently resides in Asheville, North Carolina, with his wife, Dorothy, and their two daughters, Lillian and Gwendolyn. Visit him online at www.matthewkmanning.com

ILLUSTRATOR

Scott Neely has been a professional illustrator and designer for many years. Since 1999, he's been an official Scooby-Doo and Cartoon Network artist, working on such licensed properties as Dexter's Laboratory, Johnny Bravo, Courage The Cowardly Dog, Powerpuff Girls, and more. He has also worked on Pokémon, Mickey Mouse Clubhouse, My Friends Tigger & Pooh, Handy Manny, Strawberry Shortcake, Bratz, and many other popular characters. He lives in a suburb of Philadelphia.

GLOSSARY

audible (AW-duh-buhl)—loud enough to be heard

composure (kuhm-POH-zhur)—a calm state;
self-control

deduce (di-DOOSS)—to figure something out from
clues or from what you already know

demeanor (dih-MEE-ner)—outward behavior toward
others

doppelgänger (DOP-uhl-gang-er)—someone who
looks exactly like someone else; a person's double
or alter ego

fiendish (FEEN-dish)—evil or cruel

measly (MEE-zlee)—inadequate or not very generous

portrait (POR-trit)—a drawing, painting, or
photograph of a person

ravine (ruh-VEEN)—a deep, narrow valley with
steep sides

rickety (RIK-uh-tee)—old, weak, and likely to break

suspect (suh-SPEKT)—to think that someone is
guilty with little or no proof

till (TIL)—a drawer or box in a store, used to hold
money; part of a cash register

YOU CHOOSE JOKES!

YOU CHOOSE which punch line is funniest!

Who is the busiest witch in Salem?

a. The one who works as a lights witch!

b. The one who sells witch-watches!

c. The one who tells fortunes — except that there's no future in it!

What does a wizard like best about school?

a. spelling

b. hex-am papers

c. The library — think of all the re-sorceress there!

Why was the Halloween party such a blast?

a. Dr. Frankenstein had everyone in stitches!

b. The medium raised everyone's spirits!

c. The zombie hosts loved having their friends for dinner!

But why was the other monster party such a flop?
a. The vampires were pains in the neck!
b. The mummies were all wrapped up in themselves!
c. The coffins were all board!

What do you call a ghost's mom and dad?
a. transparents
b. Mummy and Deady
c. ancest-horrors

Where did the witch go on vacation?
a. Roomania
b. Wichita
c. a dead and breakfast

How did Scooby know where the witches in Salem lived?
a. His map said, "Hex marks the spot!"
b. He saw a scary house . . . which is there! (Witches there!)
c. He looked in the newspaper ads for broom-mates.

LOOK FOR MORE . . .

← YOU CHOOSE →

SCOOBY-DOO!

THE CHOICE IS YOURS!

THE **FUN** DOESN'T STOP HERE!

DISCOVER MORE AT...

www.CAPSTONEKIDS.com

FIND COOL WEBSITES AND MORE BOOKS LIKE THIS ONE AT WWW.FACTHOUND.COM. JUST TYPE IN THE BOOK ID: 9781496543349 AND YOU'RE READY TO GO!